Usborne First Experiences
Going to School

Anne Civardi

Illustrated by Stephen Cartwright

Edited by Michelle Bates
Cover design by Neil Francis

There is a little yellow duck hiding on every double page. Can you find it?

This is the Peach family.

Mrs. Peach

Mr. Peach

Polly
Peach

Pong
the
kitten

Percy
Peach

Sidney
the gerbil

Ping
the other kitten

Dusty the cat

Percy and Polly are twins. Tomorrow they are going to school for the first time.

This is where the Peaches live.

They live above the Marsh family. Millie Marsh is going to the same school as the twins.

Mr. and Mrs. Peach wake Percy and Polly.

It is 8 o'clock in the morning. It is time for them to get ready for school. Percy and Polly get up and get dressed.

They have their breakfast.

Then the twins put on their shoes and coats. Millie is ready to go to school with them.

They all go to school.

At first, Polly is a little shy. Mrs. Todd, the teacher, says
that Mrs. Peach can stay with her for a while.

Mr. Peach hangs Percy's coat on his own special hook. He has to take Percy's pet gerbil, Sidney, back home with him.

Percy and Polly join their class.

There are lots of things to do at school such as painting, drawing, reading and dressing-up.

Some children make things out of paper, and others make things with clay. What are Percy and Polly doing?

They have fun making things.

Two of the teachers help them make tiny washing lines full of clothes to take home.

It's time for singing.

Miss Dot, the music teacher, teaches them lots of songs.
She also teaches them how to play lots of instruments.

Now it's time for a break.

At 11 o'clock, everyone has a drink and something to eat.
Percy and Polly are both very thirsty.

It's story time.

Mrs. Todd tells the children a story about a big tiger named Stripes. What is Percy up to now?

The children go out to the playground.

There are lots of things to play with outside. There are tractors and hoops, and bicycles and balls.

Polly loves going down the slide. Percy likes to play in the sand. But Millie has found something else to play with.

It's time for Percy and Polly to go home.

They have had a happy day at school and so has Millie.
They have made lots of new friends.

This edition published in 2005 by Usborne Publishing Ltd, Usborne House, 83-85 Saffron Hill, London EC1N 8RT, England.
Copyright © 2005, 1992 Usborne Publishing Ltd. www.usborne.com
First published in America in 2005. UE
The name Usborne and the devices ♀ ⊕ are Trade Marks of Usborne Publishing Ltd.

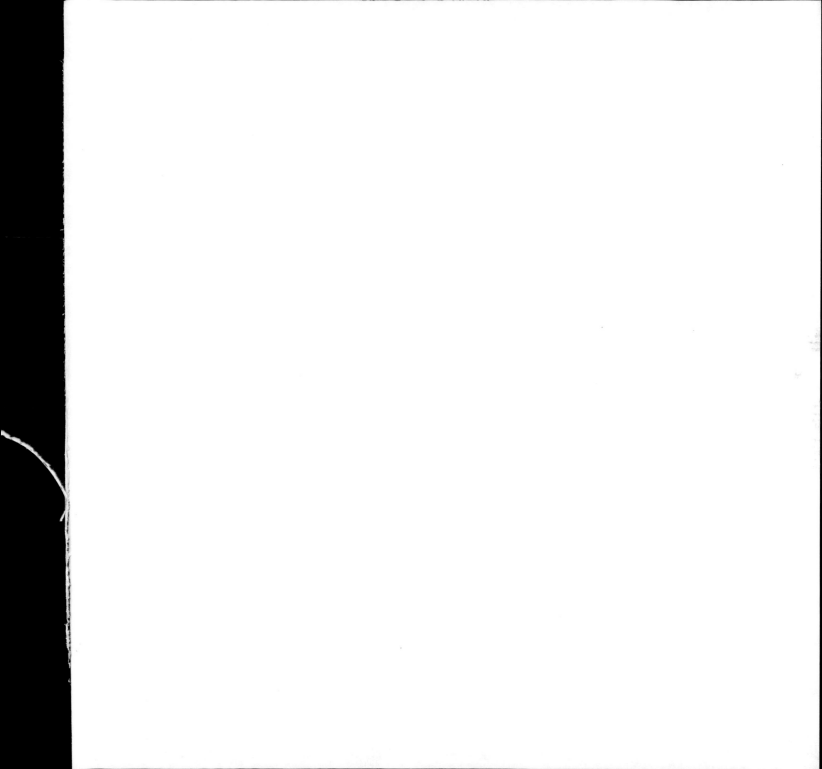